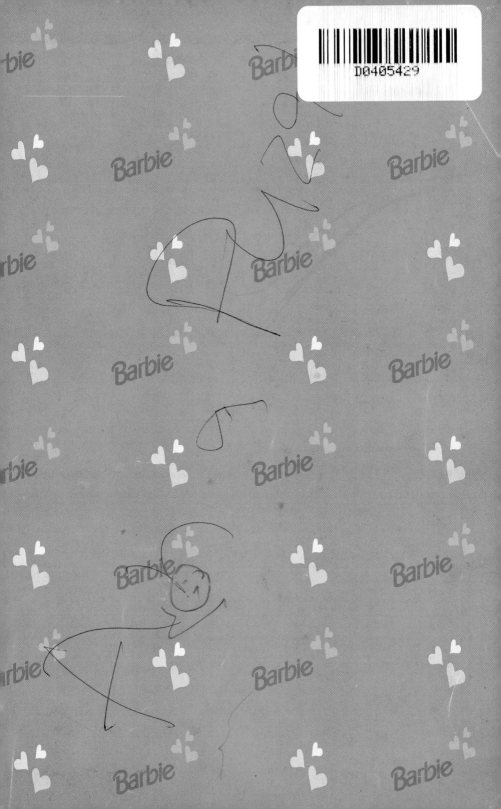

Word List

Here is a list of words that might make it easier to read this book. You'll find them in boldface the first time they appear in the story.

disappointment	dis-uh-POINT-ment
angora	ang-GOR-uh
refrigerator	ri-FRIJ-uh-ray-ter
Stegosaurus	steg-uh-SOR-uhs
eject	ee-JEKT
mischief	MIS-chif
boa	BOH-uh
detergent	di-TER-jent
disasters	di-ZAS-terz
delicate	DEL-i-kit
vacuum	VAK-yoom
overwhelmed	oh-ver-WELMD
frantically	FRAN-tik-lee
apologized	uh-POL-uh-jyzd
collapsed	kuh-LAPST
winced	winst
hairstyling	HAIR-styl-ing
imitation	im-uh-TAY-shun

Barbie™

Skipper's Baby-sitting Blues

ISBN: 0-7172-8829-3

Grolier Books

Skipper stood by the window and watched gray, gloomy clouds float slowly across the sky. "Rainy days are so boring," she sighed.

"Yeah, especially rainy Saturdays," added Stacie, her younger sister. Stacie pointed the remote control at the television and flicked through the channels. "There's nothing good on TV, either," she said glumly.

Skipper walked to the sofa and sat down beside Stacie. The two girls watched their baby sister, Kelly, happily play with a bunny on the floor.

"At least one of us doesn't seem to mind the

weather," Skipper said with a smile.

Suddenly the telephone rang. Skipper and Stacie jumped up at the same time.

"That's for me!" shouted Skipper. "I've been expecting Kevin to call."

"No, I'll bet it's Whitney for me!" Stacie exclaimed.

The two sisters giggled as they raced toward the phone. Skipper made it there first.

"Oh, hi, Ken," Skipper laughed into the phone. "Hold on while I get Barbie." She playfully stuck her tongue out at Stacie as she went up the stairs to find Barbie.

Barbie picked up the phone in her room. "Hi, Ken," Skipper heard her say. "A fifties party? Tonight? I'd love to go! I even have the perfect outfit to wear. The only problem is getting a baby-sitter for the girls. I don't think I'll be able to find someone on such short notice."

Skipper could hear the **disappointment** in

Barbie's voice. "This would be a good chance to help Barbie out," thought Skipper. "She always helps me."

Skipper went into Barbie's room. "Sis, I'd be happy to baby-sit tonight," Skipper said.

"Hold on, Ken," said Barbie. She put her hand over the receiver. "Skipper, wouldn't you rather see your friends this evening?" she asked.

"I was planning to stay home tonight," said Skipper. "Besides, we're all going to a movie together tomorrow afternoon."

"You're the greatest!" Barbie said, smiling. "Good news, Ken. It looks like I'll be able to go after all. Skipper just offered to baby-sit. See you at six-thirty."

Skipper went down to the living room and gave Stacie and Kelly a big-sisterly hug. "Did you hear that? I'm going to be your baby-sitter tonight. It'll be so great. Just the three of us!"

"You mean just the four of us," corrected

Stacie. "My friend Janet is sleeping over tonight, remember? She'll be here soon."

"The more, the merrier," said Skipper. "We can watch videos, bake cookies, listen to music."

Just then, Barbie came into the living room.

"Skipper," Barbie began, "I know you've baby-sat for Stacie and Kelly before. But taking care of two eight-year-olds *and* a toddler can be a real challenge. Janet and Stacie together can be a handful."

"Everything will be fine," said Skipper, feeling excited and confident. "I'm sixteen, you know. What could possibly go wrong?"

"Well, all right," said Barbie. "I'd better go and get ready. Ken will be here soon."

Barbie went upstairs to get dressed.

A few minutes later, the doorbell rang.

"That must be Janet!" exclaimed Stacie, racing to the door.

Stacie greeted Janet and her mother.

"Guess what, Stacie?" said Janet excitedly. "My mom let me rent *My Brother Is a Two-Headed Alien* for us to watch tonight!"

"Cool!" replied Stacie. "That one's scary!"

Barbie came downstairs in her robe. While the two girls were busy discussing the video, Barbie took Janet's mother aside.

"Do you mind if Skipper baby-sits the girls this evening?" Barbie asked. "She's sixteen, and she's very responsible."

"That seems fine to me," replied Janet's mother. Then she turned to Janet. "Remember, be on your best behavior," she said. "I'll pick you up in the morning."

"Good night, Mom," said Janet, kissing her mother good-bye.

Before long, Ken arrived to pick up Barbie. He was dressed in a gold jacket. His hair was slicked back and shiny.

"Wow!" exclaimed Skipper. "You could pass

for Elvis Presley, Ken!"

"You wouldn't say that if you heard me sing," joked Ken.

"Just wait until you see Barbie," said Stacie, coming downstairs with Janet. "She looks awesome!"

"You two are going to be the best-dressed couple at the party," Skipper added.

"Thanks," Ken said with a smile.

"Hello, handsome," called Barbie from the top of the stairs. Everyone smiled at her as she came downstairs. She was dressed in a pink **angora** sweater, a poodle skirt, bobby socks, and saddle shoes.

Ken whistled. "Barbie, you're the most!" he said.

"The most what?" asked Janet, confused.

"It's a saying from the fifties," Skipper explained. "It means she looks terrific."

"Doggie!" cried Kelly, pointing to the fabric

poodle sewn on Barbie's skirt.

Ken laughed. "Even Kelly likes your outfit, Barbie!" he said.

Barbie turned to Skipper as she and Ken were about to leave. "Remember, Skipper, you can reach me at the number on the notepad by the phone. And the emergency numbers are stuck on the **refrigerator** door. We'll be home by eleven o'clock."

"Have a great time, and don't worry!" Skipper told her. "We'll be fine."

"Thanks again for baby-sitting," said Barbie, giving Skipper a grateful hug. "See you later."

Chapter Two

As soon as Barbie and Ken had left, Stacie and Janet shouted, "Movie time!"

"I don't know about you guys, but I can't watch a movie without a big bowl of popcorn," said Skipper. "Want me to make some?"

"Great idea, Sis," said Stacie.

"Extra butter, please," added Janet.

"C'mon, Janet," said Stacie. "Let's put in the video. I can't wait to see the scene where the alien brother eats all the brussels sprouts!"

The two girls ran into the den.

Skipper carried Kelly into the kitchen and

set her down on the floor. She glanced at the clock over the stove.

"Yikes! It's past six-thirty!" Skipper cried. "It's time for your supper, Kelly. One peanut butter-and-jelly sandwich coming right up! I'll just put on the popcorn first for the girls."

She placed Kelly's stuffed bunny in front of her. "There," said Skipper, patting the toddler on the head. "Play with Mister Bunny. That should keep you out of trouble until I finish making your dinner."

Kelly giggled and clapped her hands. She picked up the stuffed animal and started to play with its floppy ears.

Skipper walked over to the kitchen cabinet and got the jar of popcorn kernels down from the shelf. Then she turned on the radio.

Just as Skipper was opening the jar, the phone rang. She ran to answer it.

"Hi, Courtney! Yeah, this is a good time to

talk. I'm baby-sitting for the girls. I'm just getting Kelly's dinner ready." Skipper started pouring the kernels into the popcorn maker. "Which new boy? Oh, you mean David. I think he's the cutest boy in our school! He asked Kim to go to the movies next Saturday?"

Skipper kept talking as she poured more kernels into the machine.

"I can't believe Kim turned him down," Skipper said. "She must be crazy!" She shut the lid on the popcorn maker and turned it on.

Then Skipper went to the pantry and took out the jars of peanut butter and jelly. She opened them up and set them on the kitchen table along with Kelly's favorite bread. As she talked to Courtney, Skipper turned back around to get a knife out of the drawer. Then she sat down on a stool.

While Skipper was talking, Kelly toddled over to the kitchen table. She stood on tiptoe,

reached up, and took down the two open jars. Skipper turned around just in time to see Kelly leaving the kitchen, but she didn't notice that the peanut butter and jelly were missing!

"Courtney, hold on a minute," said Skipper. She shouted in the direction of the den, "Kelly just walked out of the kitchen. Stacie, will you keep an eye on her while I'm in here?"

Skipper took another look at the popcorn. It was just starting to pop. "It's noisy in here," Skipper said. She held the phone tightly against one ear. "What were you saying, Court?"

Chapter Three

With the TV on in the den, it was loud in there, too. Stacie didn't hear Skipper ask her to watch Kelly.

"It's hot in here," said Janet.

"I know," said Stacie as she pushed the videotape into the VCR. "Will you turn on the fan in the window?"

"Sure," said Janet. She switched on the fan and then sat on the sofa. Barbie's cat, Nellie, jumped onto Janet's lap.

"She likes you," Stacie said. She pressed the play button on the remote control and joined Janet and Nellie on the sofa.

Stacie and Janet waited for the movie to begin, but nothing happened.

"That's strange," said Stacie. "Kelly was watching a Stanley **Stegosaurus** tape this afternoon. The VCR was working then."

"Let me try," offered Janet. Then she handed Nellie to Stacie and got up from the sofa. She pushed the rewind and play buttons a few times. But still no movie.

"That's weird," said Janet. "Maybe we should start over." She pushed the **eject** button. But the tape only partly came out of the machine.

"Try pushing it back in again," suggested Stacie. "Maybe it'll work this time."

Janet pushed the tape back into the VCR and hit play again. The girls watched the TV, hoping that the movie would start. It didn't.

"There must be something wrong with the tape," said Stacie. She gently set Nellie on a pillow and stood up. "We'd better take it out of the VCR." She pushed the eject button. But once again, the tape got stuck and came out only part of the way.

"I've got an idea," said Janet. She gave the VCR a sharp hit on its side.

"Hey, what are you doing?" exclaimed Stacie. "You could break it!"

"Well, that's what my big brother does when he has a problem with our VCR," replied Janet with a shrug.

Stacie and Janet tried to get the tape out by pressing the button several more times. But nothing worked. The tape was really stuck!

"Now what do we do?" asked Janet.

"Maybe I can pull the tape out," Stacie suggested. She grasped the edge of the tape and tugged. But it didn't budge.

"It's really jammed," said Stacie. Suddenly she had another idea. "You hold the VCR, Janet, and I'll pull on the tape as hard as I can."

Janet did as Stacie asked.

"Now, when I count to three, I'm going to pull the tape out," Stacie told her. "One. Two. THREE!"

Stacie pulled hard on the tape. Suddenly she toppled backward.

"Yikes!" Stacie cried.

She landed on the sofa right on top of Nellie. With a frightened hiss, Nellie leapt off the pillow, tearing it with her claws. As Stacie scrambled to her feet, feathers spilled out of the pillow. Before the girls knew it, the fan was blowing feathers everywhere!

"The fan!" shouted Stacie. Janet hurried through the blizzard of feathers to the window. After fumbling with the switch for a moment, she managed to turn off the fan.

The girls looked around in amazement. Tiny white feathers covered the carpet, sofa, and chairs.

Stacie and Janet took one look at each other and burst out laughing.

Just then, Janet held up the tape. "Look, Stacie! Your idea worked after all!"

The tape was out of the VCR!

Meanwhile, Skipper was finishing up her phone call with Courtney. "I'd better go," Skipper said. "It's time for Kelly's dinner. I'll see you tomorrow at the movies."

Skipper hung up the phone. When she turned around to make the sandwich, Skipper gasped in shock. The lid of the overfilled popcorn maker had come off. Popcorn was everywhere!

"Oh, no!" Skipper cried. She quickly unplugged the machine. "Just look at this mess!" She turned off the radio and went to the laundry room to get a broom and dustpan. Just as she was about to start sweeping, Stacie and Janet appeared in the doorway. They took one look at the popcorn-covered floor and broke into giggles.

"This isn't funny," said Skipper, trying to keep a straight face. But after a moment, all three girls were doubled over with laughter.

"I could use some help cleaning up this mess," Skipper said at last. "Start sweeping while I get the garbage pail."

As Skipper handed Stacie the broom, she noticed something in Stacie's hair. "Where did this come from?" she asked, holding up a tiny white feather.

"It's a long story, Sis," Stacie said slowly.

"Yeah," Janet giggled. "It's about a cat, a feather pillow, and a fan."

"Oh, no," said Skipper, trying to stay calm.

"Oh, yes," said Stacie, taking Skipper's arm and leading the way.

The girls started to walk back to the den. But when they reached the hallway, all three froze.

"Oh, Kelly!" cried Skipper, running past the den to the end of the hallway.

There was Kelly, sitting on the floor in the hallway. She was covered in sticky peanut butter and jelly from head to toe. Baby-size purple and brown handprints were smeared all over the wall!

"Kelly paint!" she declared, pointing to the wall and grinning.

Chapter Four

"Stacie, you were supposed to be watching Kelly," Skipper said, turning to her sister.

"But she was in the kitchen with you," replied Stacie, looking confused.

"Didn't you hear me call from the kitchen?" asked Skipper.

"I'm really sorry, Skipper. I didn't hear anything," replied Stacie.

Skipper shook her head. "Well, we're just lucky that Kelly is all right," she said. "I guess the messes in the kitchen and den will have to wait." She scooped up Kelly in her arms. "I'd better clean you up, little one. After that, we'll give dinner another try. You must be really hungry by now."

"Kelly want cookie," said the messy toddler.

"Don't worry, Skipper. We'll clean up the walls in no time," said Stacie.

"Let's get a bucket of warm, soapy water and some sponges," added Janet.

Skipper smiled warmly at the girls. "Thanks. That would be a big help. We need to get this place cleaned up before Barbie comes home."

Skipper carried Kelly upstairs. But as she was passing Barbie's room, the phone rang. She hurried into Barbie's bedroom and picked it up.

"Hello?" said Skipper. "Oh, hi, Christie. I'm fine, just a little busy right now. What do you need? Someone's phone number? No problem. Hold on a minute. I have to go downstairs, where Barbie keeps her phone book. I'll be right back."

Then Skipper set Kelly down on the floor

by the closet.

"Stay right there, young lady," Skipper told the toddler. "You've gotten into enough **mischief** for one night."

Skipper ran downstairs and returned with Barbie's phone book. After a few seconds, she found the number and gave it to Christie. She was just hanging up when Stacie and Janet came into the room.

"Uh-oh, Skipper!" said Stacie. "We have a problem."

Skipper looked at them. "What's happened now?" she asked her sister.

Stacie pointed to Barbie's closet. Skipper looked over and gasped.

"Kelly pretty!" Kelly said, grinning.

The food-covered toddler had managed to put on one of Barbie's dresses. She was wearing a polka-dotted hat on her head and a pink feather **boa**. On her feet, Kelly wore a pair of Barbie's high heels.

She stood surrounded by some blouses, scarves, and shoes that she had pulled out of the closet.

"Oh, no!" cried Skipper. "I only had my back turned for a minute. How can someone so small make such a big mess?"

But Kelly looked so cute that the older girls couldn't help laughing.

"We'd better start cleaning all of this up," said Skipper finally. She bent over and gathered up some of the clothing.

Suddenly Skipper dropped the pile and looked at her hands. "Yuck!" she exclaimed, wrinkling her nose in disgust. "There's peanut butter and jelly all over these clothes!"

"Look at Barbie's beautiful dress!" Stacie cried as she took the dress off Kelly. "It's covered with grape jelly!"

"It sure is going to take a lot of **detergent** to get all this stuff clean," Janet declared, shaking her head.

"Are hats washable?" asked Stacie. She held the sticky hat carefully between her thumb and index finger.

"How about feather boas?" asked Janet, making a face.

"I'll have to wash those by hand with soap and water," replied Skipper, rolling up her sleeves. "Guys, will each of you please take some of the messy clothing down to the laundry room? I'll deal with Kelly."

Skipper scooped up the toddler in her arms. "I think we've had enough dress-up fun for one evening, young lady," she said.

Then Skipper turned to Stacie and Janet. "And you guys need to eat, too. How about ordering Chinese food? Is that okay with both of you?"

"Sure, anything but peanut butter and jelly," Stacie replied with a laugh.

Skipper laughed, too. "Watch your step as you carry the laundry downstairs," she told them. "We've had enough **disasters** for one night."

"I think we've had enough disasters for a whole *year!*" added Stacie.

Chapter Five

Stacie and Janet each carried some of Barbie's clothes past the kitchen to the laundry room. Skipper followed close behind, holding Kelly. The girls carefully placed the clothing in the washing machine.

"Here, let me measure the detergent," said Skipper. She put down Kelly, poured out a cup of soap powder, and emptied it into the machine. She turned the knob to the **delicate** cycle and started the machine.

"What should we do next?" asked Stacie.

"Well, let's see," Skipper began. "There's

popcorn all over the kitchen, feathers all over the den, and peanut butter and jelly all over Barbie's bedroom. Where should we begin?"

"I say we run away and never come back!" Stacie joked.

Skipper sighed. "Why don't you two work on cleaning up the feathers? I'll order our dinner and feed and bathe Kelly. Then you can start sweeping up the popcorn while I clean up Barbie's room."

"Sounds good to me," said Stacie. "C'mon, Janet. I'll race you to the den!" The girls hurried off.

Skipper carried Kelly into the kitchen. She held Kelly over the sink and washed off her hands and face. "That will do for now, little one," she said to Kelly. "After your dinner, we'll give you a bath and get you really clean." Then Skipper crunched through the popcorn on the floor to the refrigerator to get an egg and the butter.

"Well, Kelly, I hope you're in the mood for a scrambled egg and toast," said Skipper. "We're out of peanut butter and jelly right now."

Meanwhile, Stacie and Janet were struggling to get the **vacuum** cleaner out of the hall closet.

"Boy, this sure is a big vacuum!" huffed Janet, tugging on the base of the machine.

"It's a Snarf-it 2000," Stacie told her, pulling on the handle. "It's powerful enough to suck up a bowling ball."

"I'll remember that the next time I want to vacuum up some bowling balls!" teased Janet. Suddenly she stopped tugging on the machine. "Wait a minute, Stacie." Janet pointed up at a low shelf piled with large envelopes. "I think the handle is caught on that shelf. Maybe we should take down those envelopes in case they fall. What's in them, anyway?"

"It's okay, Janet," Stacie grunted in between tugs. "If I just pull on the vacuum a little harder, I'll get it out. Anyway, those envelopes are just stuffed with old photos."

Stacie yanked on the vacuum with all her might. The vacuum cleaner was pulled free, but the shelf tipped over. The envelopes, and the photos inside them, showered down on the two girls.

"Oh, no!" Janet groaned. "What else could go wrong?"

"Don't ask," Stacie warned. "I'll put all this stuff back in the closet. It shouldn't take too long."

"And I'll get started on the vacuuming," suggested Janet.

"Thanks," Stacie smiled. "I'll be in to help you in a few minutes."

Janet pushed the vacuum cleaner into the den and began to clean up the feathers. As she was vacuuming, she thought she heard the washing machine buzzer go off. "I'd better go and check the wash. Stacie has enough to do," Janet thought. She turned off the vacuum and ran to the laundry room. The washing machine was still going.

"That's weird. I was sure I heard a buzzer,"

Janet said to herself. She opened the washing machine lid and looked inside. "Hmm. Barbie's clothes sure were filthy. Maybe I'd better add a little more detergent to make sure that they get *really* clean."

Janet measured out a cup of powder and sprinkled it into the machine. "That should do it," she said with a smile.

Meanwhile, Stacie had almost finished gathering up the photos. She really wanted to stop and look at some of them, but she knew she should help Janet clean up the den. She was putting away the last few pictures when Skipper walked by with Kelly.

"What happened here?" Skipper asked, looking surprised.

"You don't want to know," replied Stacie with a sigh.

"Are you and Janet okay?" Skipper asked.

"We're fine. We just had another little

accident," explained Stacie.

"I wish I could help, but Kelly still needs her bath. Plus, it's already past her bedtime," said Skipper.

"It's okay," said Stacie. "I'm almost finished. Besides, you have one super-sticky little girl on your hands."

Skipper laughed. "No kidding! Look, I'll be upstairs with Kelly if you need me. Dinner should be here soon."

As Skipper went upstairs, Stacie thought about Barbie's messy clothing. "Gee, I wonder if Skipper put enough detergent in the machine," she said to herself. "After all, those clothes were *covered* with peanut butter and jelly." Stacie put the last of the photos in an envelope and placed all the envelopes back on the shelf. She could hear Janet vacuuming in the den as she went to the laundry room.

After Stacie had added more detergent, she

hurried to join Janet in the den. All of the feathers had been vacuumed up.

"Well, at least the den doesn't look like a pillow factory anymore!" exclaimed Stacie. "You've done a great job, Janet."

"Thanks to the trusty Snarf-it 2000," said Janet, proudly patting the vacuum cleaner. "No home should be without one."

"Should we give Skipper a hand with the popcorn?" asked Stacie. "I'm sure she would appreciate our help."

"Of course," replied Janet cheerfully. "That is, if you think the Snarf-it 2000 will clean up popcorn as well as it does bowling balls!"

"I think a broom will do just fine!" said Stacie.

Both girls laughed as they ran off to tackle the mess in the kitchen.

Chapter Six

On their way to the kitchen, Janet and Stacie heard the doorbell ring. They raced to the front door and looked out the window.

"Skipper, the delivery man is here with the food," shouted Stacie.

"Tell him to wait a minute," Skipper shouted back. "I need to go to my room to get money. I'll be right there. Come on, honey bunny," she cooed to Kelly as she carried her in her arms.

"Just a minute, please," Stacie called to the delivery man through the door.

"Hey, Janet, did I ever tell you about that

web site where you can order videos at half price?" Stacie asked Janet.

"No," replied Janet. "But it sounds cool! Maybe my mom will let me buy my own copy of *My Brother Is a Two-Headed Alien*."

"C'mon, let's go up to my room," Stacie said.

"Shouldn't we clean up the kitchen first?" asked Janet.

"Looking on the Internet will only take a minute," replied Stacie.

"Okay," said Janet, and the girls quickly headed upstairs.

When they popped their heads into the nursery, Skipper was getting a squirming Kelly into her pajamas. "I'll get that money in a minute, Stacie," said Skipper.

Just then the phone rang.

"Now, who could that be?" wondered Skipper. She still had a lot of cleaning up to do, and the man was waiting downstairs with their food. She really didn't have time to chat.

"Kelly down!" said Kelly.

"No way!" Skipper laughed. "I'm not letting you out of my sight for a second!" With Kelly in her arms, Skipper hurried to the phone in Barbie's room. "Hello? Oh, Barbie! I wasn't expecting to hear from you," said Skipper.

"How's it going?" Barbie asked.

"Great! Couldn't be better!" Skipper replied a little too cheerfully. "How's the party?"

"We're having a great time," said Barbie. "I'm so glad I could go. You should see Ken. I think he's really starting to believe he's Elvis Presley!"

"That's great, Sis," said Skipper, forcing a laugh. "So you'll be staying for a while longer, I mess? I mean, I *guess.*"

"We're planning to leave in about an hour. Skipper, is everything all right?" asked Barbie.

"All right?" Skipper said with a nervous

laugh. "Of course everything is all right. Why wouldn't it be all right?" she blurted out.

"Well, you sound a little out of breath," replied Barbie, with a note of concern in her voice.

"Oh, I just ran upstairs to answer the phone," Skipper answered.

"Isn't the phone downstairs working?" asked Barbie.

Skipper heard the doorbell ring again. "Uh, sure it is. Everything's great here. Really. Got to go!" Skipper hung up the phone.

Just then she heard a distressing *meow* from downstairs.

"Now what?" Skipper cried, feeling totally **overwhelmed.**

Still holding Kelly in her arms, Skipper went downstairs. "Nellie? Here, Nel!" she called.

Skipper hurried into the living room and looked around but couldn't see Nellie anywhere. Then she rushed into the den. She was glad to see that Janet and Stacie had been able to clean up all the feathers. Then she heard another loud *meow!* It seemed to be coming from the kitchen.

"Nellie go meow!" shouted Kelly.

"I know, sweetie. It sounds like she's in trouble," said Skipper. She started to walk toward the kitchen but stopped in her tracks. There was a mountain of soapsuds spilling out of the laundry room and flowing through the kitchen door!

Skipper carefully waded through the suds and glanced into the kitchen. There, stranded on a counter, was poor Nellie. She was looking down nervously at the sea of soapsuds and floating popcorn that covered the floor. The fur along her back was standing straight up.

"Kelly play with bubbles!" shouted Kelly.

"No, Kelly," Skipper said firmly. "Let's go find Stacie so she can keep an eye on you while I try to straighten this out."

Ding, dong! rang the doorbell.

"And I've got to get the door!" cried Skipper. She hurried to the foot of the stairs and **frantically** called up to her sister.

"Sorry, Skipper. We got busy with the computer," Stacie **apologized** as she and Janet came running downstairs. "We're all set to help clean up the popcorn."

Stacie stopped short when she saw Skipper's face. "You look awful. What's wrong?" she asked.

"Here," Skipper said quickly as she handed Kelly over to Stacie. "Watch Kelly for me. The washing machine is out of control! Nellie is stranded on the kitchen counter!"

The doorbell rang again.

"And our dinner is at the front door!" exclaimed Skipper. "Just one more minute!" she called to the delivery man.

Skipper dashed off toward the kitchen. She made her way through the suds to Nellie and gathered up the frightened cat in her arms. Then she slipped and slid into the laundry room and turned off the washing machine.

"Gee, how could the washing machine overflow?" Skipper wondered out loud as she hurried into the living room where Janet and Stacie were playing with Kelly. "I just don't get it. I measured the detergent so carefully!"

Stacie and Janet looked at each other. "I added some more," Janet confessed.

"You?" exclaimed Stacie. "I added some more, too!"

"Oh, no," groaned Skipper, covering her face with her hands. "Why didn't you ask me first?"

"Well, you were busy with Kelly," said Stacie.

"And Barbie's clothes were so dirty," added Janet.

"We're really sorry, Skipper. We were just trying to help," Stacie said quietly.

"I know. It's not your fault," said Skipper gently. "Things are just going all wrong tonight."

She stroked Nellie's back. The cat purred in her arms as the doorbell rang again. "Okay, I'll get the door. Then I'll put Kelly to bed. Why don't you two see what you can do with the laundry room?" said a worn-out Skipper.

"Sure, Sis. Whatever we can do to help," Stacie replied.

Suddenly the girls heard a voice from the doorway say, "You all look as though you've had quite an evening!"

Chapter Seven

"Barbie!" the three girls exclaimed.

Barbie stood in the doorway smiling, with Ken at her side. He was holding boxes of Chinese food.

"Skipper, I sensed that something might be wrong from the sound of your voice over the phone," Barbie explained. "I thought I'd better come home a little early in case you needed help."

Skipper rushed over to her older sister and fell into her arms. Stacie and Janet **collapsed** on the sofa with Kelly.

"Oh, Barbie," Skipper groaned, "I don't know where to begin."

"Just as I thought," Barbie said with a gentle laugh. She gave Skipper a warm hug. "Okay, you can tell me all about it. But first you all need to eat. And little Kelly here needs to go to bed."

"Kelly want story!" piped up the toddler, yawning.

"All right," said Barbie. "But only a short one tonight."

"Thanks, Sis," Skipper called as Barbie carried Kelly upstairs to her bedroom.

Ken headed for the kitchen to set the table for dinner. "You ladies must be starving," he said.

"We are!" shouted Skipper, Stacie, and Janet at the same time.

"In fact," Skipper said, steering Ken away from the soap bubbles in the kitchen, "let's save time and just eat in the living room."

When they had finished eating, Barbie came downstairs and joined them.

"So, what happened, Skipper? And why was

that poor man waiting at the door?" asked Barbie.

Skipper began to tell Barbie what had happened. But she left out some parts.

"You forgot about when Janet and I added more soap powder to the washing machine. And then it overflowed," Stacie said helpfully.

"Or how about when Kelly played dress-up with Barbie's clothes?" added Janet.

Skipper gave Stacie and Janet a look. "I was getting to that part."

"What happened to my clothes?" Barbie asked, looking nervously from Janet to Skipper.

"Well," Skipper began, "you see, Kelly got some of her dinner on your pink dress."

"My favorite pink dress?" Barbie exclaimed. She **winced** at the thought of the pretty fabric covered with sticky peanut butter and jelly.

"Don't forget about the blouses and the feather boa," added Stacie.

Barbie looked at Skipper. "So the clothing in

the washing machine is all mine?" she asked slowly.

Skipper nodded. "I'm sorry, Barbie."

Barbie smiled and shook her head. "Well, I'm sure everything will be all right. The most important thing is that no one was hurt," she said, playfully messing up Skipper's hair. "Don't be too hard on yourself, Skipper. We all have days when nothing seems to go right."

"I've really learned my lesson," declared Skipper. "I'll never try to handle too many things at once again. And I'll *never ever* turn my back on a toddler!"

Barbie smiled at her sister. "Hey, did I ever tell you about the time my friend Midge came over when I was baby-sitting you and Stacie?" she said.

"No. What happened?" Skipper asked.

"Well, I was about your age, Skipper, and you were about Stacie's age," Barbie began.

"How old was I?" Stacie asked.

"Not much older than Kelly," replied Barbie.

"Anyway, Midge came over to keep me company. We started to watch a television program about **hairstyling** tips. Skipper, you were sitting on the rug watching the program with us. Stacie was playing beside you. Well, Midge and I were trying out the hairstyles on each other, and I turned my back for just a minute."

"That sounds familiar!" Skipper said with a laugh.

"Well, the next thing I knew," continued Barbie, turning to Skipper, "you had decided that Stacie needed a haircut."

"Oh, no!" Skipper exclaimed, laughing.

Barbie chuckled. "Skipper, you had cut off Stacie's lovely, blond pigtails and taped them onto your doll's head!"

"So that's why I have a really short haircut in all the pictures taken at my second birthday party!" cried Stacie, playfully punching Skipper.

"Well, at least no one's hair got chopped

off while *I* was baby-sitting," Skipper joked.

"Luckily, Stacie's hair grew back," said Barbie. "But from that day on, I took baby-sitting much more seriously."

"Don't worry, this will never happen again," Skipper told Barbie. "And I promise to clean up the mess."

"Little lady," said Ken, doing his Elvis Presley **imitation,** "I'd be honored to assist you."

"Sure, Elvis. Feel free to pitch in!" Skipper said with a laugh.

"We'll get ready for bed," said Stacie. "C'mon, Janet. Let's watch *My Brother Is a Two-Headed Alien* in the morning. I'm too tired to be scared to death right now!"

"Good night, everyone," said the girls as they headed up the stairs.

Skipper, Barbie, and Ken turned toward the kitchen to start cleaning up.

"Well," said Barbie, "there's one good thing

about all of this."

"What's that, Sis?" Skipper asked.

Barbie's eyes sparkled. "I'll have enough clean clothes for a month!"